MIKE MULLIGAN
and More

MIKE MULLIGAN
and More

A Virginia Lee Burton Treasury

HOUGHTON MIFFLIN COMPANY
Boston 2002

www.houghtonmifflinbooks.com

Library of Congress Cataloging-in-Publication Data is available for this title.

ISBN 0-618-25627-X

Printed in Singapore
TWP 10 9 8 7 6 5 4 3 2 1

Introduction

VIRGINIA LEE BURTON BELIEVED IN CHILDREN. For her, preparing a new book meant getting children's input in the early stages of creation. She would often gather up her two young sons and their friends, offer ample portions of hot cocoa and cookies, and then watch their reactions while she read the story aloud. If the youngsters lost interest and began to fidget, she later commented, "It was back to the typewriter, back to the drawing board."

As a result, *Mike Mulligan and His Steam Shovel, The Little House, Katy and the Big Snow,* and *Maybelle the Cable Car* are solidly built stories with well-integrated text and images. They evince her intense belief that stories written for children should be loved by children. That idea has proved valid: written five to six decades ago, these books not only continue to appeal to children but also remain, permanently etched, in the minds and hearts of adults who have read them in childhood. The author Ann Tyler says, "I have returned to *The Little House* over and over, sinking into its colorful, complicated pictures all through childhood and adolescence and adulthood," and the television talk-show host Jay Leno mentions *Mike Mulligan and His Steam Shovel* as a shaping force in his career as a comic.

Born in Newton Center, Massachusetts, in 1909, Burton spent most of her childhood and adolescence in California. In 1928, she returned to the East, planning to join her sister's traveling dance troupe. However, when her father broke his leg, Virginia stayed behind to care for him: "That was the beginning and end of my dancing career, which was just as well, because I wasn't very good, anyway."

The accident proved fortuitous for the world of children's books. Virginia abandoned thoughts of a career on stage and instead channeled her artistic talents into drawing and illustration. She worked for a time at the *Boston Transcript* newspaper, attending theatrical and sporting events. From a seat in the audience she sketched participating personalities, learning to capture the human form quickly and skillfully. A job teaching children art at the YMCA brought understanding of children's interests and needs. She later incorporated both of these experiences into her books.

After a friend suggested she enroll in a figure drawing class at the Boston Museum of Art taught by the highly regarded George Demetrios, Virginia's life took a decided turn. Six months later, in a happy turn of events, she married her teacher. The couple soon settled in Folly Cove in what was then—and is still to some extent—an isolated area on Cape Ann. Folly Cove nurtured Jinnee, as she was called, on several levels. There, she fostered close relationships within her family, developed ties with the local artist community, drew strength from living intimately with nature, and found inspiration for her work. Those who knew Jinnee speak of the joy that radiated from her life—a joy, it seems, that infected everyone who came in contact with her.

Important in her personal life, place played a major role in her books as well. *Mike Mulligan and His Steam Shovel*, for example, is set in Popperville—a place so real that children's letters to the publisher ask for directions to the village. In reality, Popperville is based on West Newbury, Massachusetts, a place Virginia often visited and whose town hall provided the model for the building under construction in the story.

In *Katy and the Big Snow*, Burton used Gloucester as her fictional Geoppolis. She created a pictorial double-page map of Geoppolis for the book, but those familiar with Gloucester will find distinguishing landmarks. *Maybelle the Cable Car*, of course, is set in San Francisco, a tribute to a place well remembered and loved, where Virginia studied art and dance. Published in 1952, the book was dedicated to Mrs. Hans Klussman for being "a leading light" in the battle to save the cable cars from extinction.

Place, perhaps, played the biggest role in Burton's *The Little House*. When she and her husband bought their home in Folly Cove, they thought it too close to the highway and had it moved several hundred feet back into an apple orchard. That experience, Burton tells, stimulated the writing of *The Little House*. Children and adults alike respond to the story. A small pink house, beloved by several generations, gradually suffers the indignities of urban sprawl and becomes bedraggled and boarded until it is finally rescued and happily returned to a pastoral setting. *The Little House* won the prestigious Caldecott Medal in 1942 for its outstanding contribution to children's literature and has stayed in print for its entire sixty years. Like all of Burton's books, it is grounded in the author's innate enthusiasm and glows under her artistic polish.

Though not included in this compilation, *Choo Choo: The Story of the Engine Who Ran Away* also has roots in Burton's family life. The idea for the story came, Burton once revealed, while taking her eldest son, Aris, then five, to watch the switching of the railroad cars at nearby Rockport Station. Her last book, *Life Story*, which she worked on for eight years, is another book that exemplifies the close connections Burton made with the world around her. In the course of presenting an illustrated, geologic history of the world, Burton devoted the last twenty pages to her Folly Cove home, where a seasonal cycle shows the family planting a garden, tending the yard, gathering apples, and shoveling snow. They also find the author at her drawing board and reading under the apple tree. The book closes with, "And now it is your Life Story and it is you who play the leading role. The stage is set, the time is now, and the place wherever you are. Each passing second is a new link in the endless chain of Time. The drama of Life is a continuous story—ever new, ever changing, and ever wondrous to behold." As in the other twelve books she illustrated, Burton offers hope and comfort and joy in life. The messages she gave are as real and meaningful today as they were when written so many decades ago.

—*Barbara Elleman*

MIKE MULLIGAN

AND HIS STEAM SHOVEL

MIKE MULLIGAN
AND HIS
STEAM SHOVEL

STORY AND PICTURES BY VIRGINIA LEE BURTON

HOUGHTON MIFFLIN COMPANY · BOSTON

TO

MIKE

Mike Mulligan had a steam shovel,
  a beautiful red steam shovel.
    Her name was Mary Anne.
      Mike Mulligan was very proud of Mary Anne.
        He always said that she could dig as much in a day
          as a hundred men could dig in a week,
            but he had never been quite sure
              that this was true.

Mike Mulligan and Mary Anne
had been digging together
for years and years.
Mike Mulligan took such good care
of Mary Anne
she never grew old.

It was Mike Mulligan and Mary Anne
    and some others
  who dug the great canals
    for the big boats
      to sail through.

20

It was Mike Mulligan
and Mary Anne
and some others
who cut through
the high mountains
so that trains
could go through.

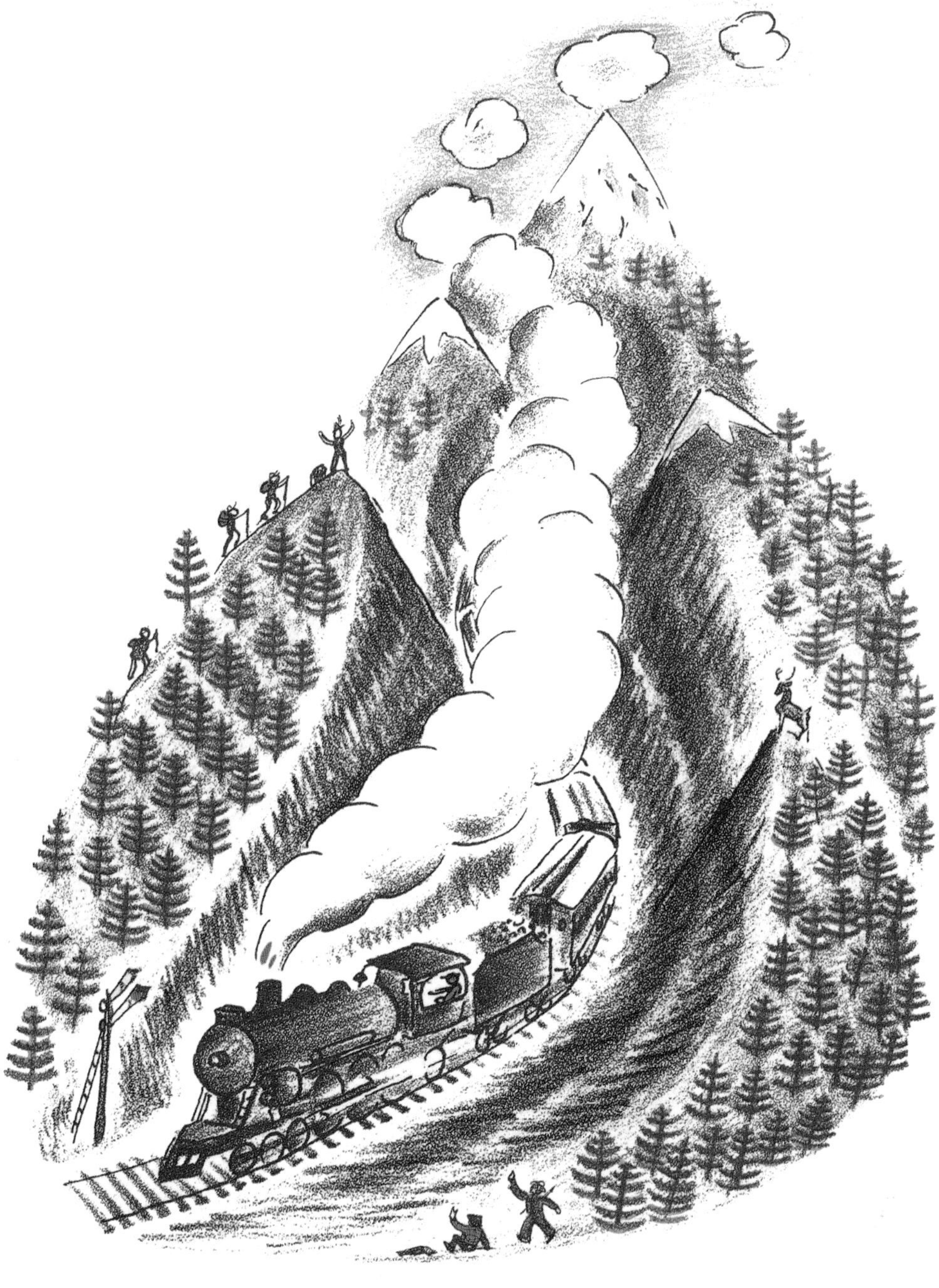

It was Mike Mulligan and Mary Anne
and some others
who lowered the hills
and straightened the curves

to make the long highways
for the automobiles.

It was Mike Mulligan
and Mary Anne
and some others
who smoothed out the ground
and filled in the holes

to make the landing fields
for the airplanes.

26

And it was Mike Mulligan
and Mary Anne
and some others
who dug the deep holes
for the cellars
of the tall skyscrapers
in the big cities.
When people used to stop
and watch them,
Mike Mulligan and Mary Anne
used to dig a little faster
and a little better.
The more people stopped,
the faster and better they dug.
Some days they would keep
as many as thirty-seven trucks
busy taking away the dirt they had dug.

Then along came
the new gasoline shovels
and the new electric shovels
and the new Diesel motor shovels
and took all the jobs away from the steam shovels.

Mike Mulligan

and Mary Anne

were

VERY

SAD.

All the other steam shovels were being sold for junk,
or left out in old gravel pits to rust and fall apart.
Mike loved Mary Anne.   He couldn't do that to her.

He had taken
such good care of her
that she could still dig
as much in a day
as a hundred men
could dig in a week;
at least he thought she could
but he wasn't quite sure.
Everywhere they went
the new gas shovels
and the new electric shovels
and the new Diesel motor shovels
had all the jobs.   No one wanted
Mike Mulligan and Mary Anne any more.
Then one day Mike read in a newspaper that the town
of Popperville was going to build a new town hall.
'We are going to dig the cellar of that town hall,'
said Mike to Mary Anne, and off they started.

They left the canals
and the railroads
and the highways
and the airports
and the big cities
where no one wanted them any more
and went away out in the country.

They crawled along slowly
up the hills and down the hills
till they came to the little town
of Popperville.

When they got there they found that the selectmen
were just deciding who should dig the cellar for the new town hall.
Mike Mulligan spoke to Henry B. Swap, one of the selectmen.
'I heard,' he said, 'that you are going
to build a new town hall.   Mary Anne and I
will dig the cellar for you in just one day.'
'What!' said Henry B. Swap.   'Dig a cellar in a day!
It would take a hundred men at least a week
to dig the cellar for our new town hall.'
'Sure,' said Mike, 'but Mary Anne can dig as much in a day
as a hundred men can dig in a week.'
Though he had never been quite sure that this was true.
Then he added,
'If we can't do it, you won't have to pay.'
Henry B. Swap thought that this would be
an easy way to get part of the cellar dug for nothing,
so he smiled in rather a mean way
and gave the job of digging the cellar of the new town hall
to Mike Mulligan and Mary Anne.

They started in
early the next morning
just as the sun was coming up.
Soon a little boy came along.
'Do you think you will finish by sundown?'
he said to Mike Mulligan.
'Sure,' said Mike, 'if you stay and watch us.
We always work faster and better
when someone is watching us.'
So the little boy stayed to watch.

Then Mrs. McGillicuddy,
Henry B. Swap,
and the Town Constable
came over to see
what was happening,
and they stayed to watch.

Mike Mulligan
and Mary Anne
dug a little faster
and a little better.

This gave the little boy a good idea.

He ran off and told the postman with the morning mail,

the telegraph boy on his bicycle,

the milkman with his cart and horse,

the doctor on his way home,

and the farmer and his family

coming into town for the day,

and they all stopped and stayed to watch.

That made Mike Mulligan and Mary Anne

dig a little faster and a little better.

They finished the first corner

neat and square . . .

but the sun was getting higher.

FARM MACHINERY—SEEDS
SEWING MACHINES—
DRY GOODS—GROCERYS
PLUMMING FIXTURES
FEED - HARDWARE
SILAS ZINK...PROPRIETOR
GENERAL STORE

Clang! Clang! Clang!

The Fire Department arrived.

They had seen the smoke

and thought there was a fire.

Then the little boy said,

'Why don't you stay and watch?'

So the Fire Department of Popperville

stayed to watch Mike Mulligan and Mary Anne.

When they heard the fire engine, the children

in the school across the street couldn't keep

their eyes on their lessons.   The teacher called

a long recess and the whole school came out to watch.

That made Mike Mulligan and Mary Anne

dig still faster and still better.

They finished the second corner neat and square,
   but the sun was right up in the top of the sky.

43

Now the girl who answers
the telephone called up the next towns
of Bangerville and Bopperville and
Kipperville and Kopperville and told them
what was happening in Popperville.
All the people came over to see
if Mike Mulligan and his steam shovel
could dig the cellar in just one day.
The more people came, the faster
Mike Mulligan and Mary Anne dug.
But they would have to hurry.
They were only halfway through
and the sun was beginning to go down.

They finished the third corner . . . neat and square.

Never had Mike Mulligan and Mary Anne
had so many people to watch them;
never had they dug so fast and so well;
and never had the sun seemed
to go down so fast.
'Hurry, Mike Mulligan!
Hurry! Hurry!'
shouted the little boy.
'There's not much more time!'
Dirt was flying everywhere,
and the smoke and steam were so thick
that the people could hardly see anything.
But listen!

Bing! Bang! Crash! Slam!
Louder and Louder,
Faster and
Faster.

47

Then suddenly it was quiet.
Slowly the dirt settled down.
The smoke and steam cleared away,
and there was the cellar
all finished.

Four corners . . . neat and square;
four walls . . . straight down,
and Mike Mulligan and Mary Anne at the bottom,
and the sun was just going down behind the hill.
'Hurray!' shouted the people.   'Hurray for Mike Mulligan
and his steam shovel!   They have dug the cellar in just one day.'

Suddenly the little boy said,
  'How are they going to get out?'
    'That's right,' said Mrs. McGillicuddy
      to Henry B. Swap. 'How is he going
        to get his steam shovel out?'
          Henry B. Swap didn't answer,
            but he smiled in rather a mean way.
            Then everybody said,
              'How are they going to get out?
              'Hi! Mike Mulligan!
                How are you going to get
                  your steam shovel out?'

50

Mike Mulligan
looked around
at the four square walls
and four square corners,
and he said,
'We've dug so fast
and we've dug so well
that we've quite forgotten
to leave a way out!'
Nothing like this had ever happened
to Mike Mulligan and Mary Anne before,
and they didn't know what to do.

51

Nothing like this
        had ever happened before
        in Popperville.
    Everybody started
talking at once,
        and everybody had
        a different idea,
        and everybody thought
    that his idea was the best.
They talked and they talked
        and they argued and they fought
        till they were worn out,
        and still no one knew how to get
    Mike Mulligan and Mary Anne
    out of the cellar they had dug.
    Then Henry B. Swap said,
    'The job isn't finished because
Mary Anne isn't out of the cellar,
so Mike Mulligan won't get paid.'
And he smiled again in a rather mean way.

Now the little boy,
who had been keeping very quiet,
had another good idea.
He said,
'Why couldn't we leave Mary Anne in the cellar
and build the new town hall above her?
Let her be the furnace for the new town hall *
and let Mike Mulligan be the janitor.
Then you wouldn't have to buy a new furnace,
and we could pay Mike Mulligan
for digging the cellar
in just one day.'

53

* Acknowledgments to Dickie Birkenbush.

'Why not?' said Henry B. Swap,
   and smiled in a way
      that was not quite so mean.
      'Why not?' said Mrs. McGillicuddy.
      'Why not?' said the Town Constable.
      'Why not?' said all the people.
      So they found a ladder
         and climbed down into the cellar
            to ask Mike Mulligan and Mary Anne.

'Why not?' said Mike Mulligan.
So it was decided,
    and everybody was happy.

They built the new town hall
right over Mike Mulligan and Mary Anne.
It was finished before winter.

Every day the little boy goes over to see
Mike Mulligan and Mary Anne,
and Mrs. McGillicuddy takes him
nice hot apple pies.   As for Henry B. Swap,
he spends most of his time in the cellar
of the new town hall listening to the stories
that Mike Mulligan has to tell
and smiling in a way that isn't mean at all.

Now when you go to Popperville,
be sure to go down in the cellar
    of the new town hall.
    There they'll be,
        Mike Mulligan and Mary Anne . . .
        Mike in his rocking chair
            smoking his pipe,
        and Mary Anne beside him,
            warming up the meetings
            in the new town hall.

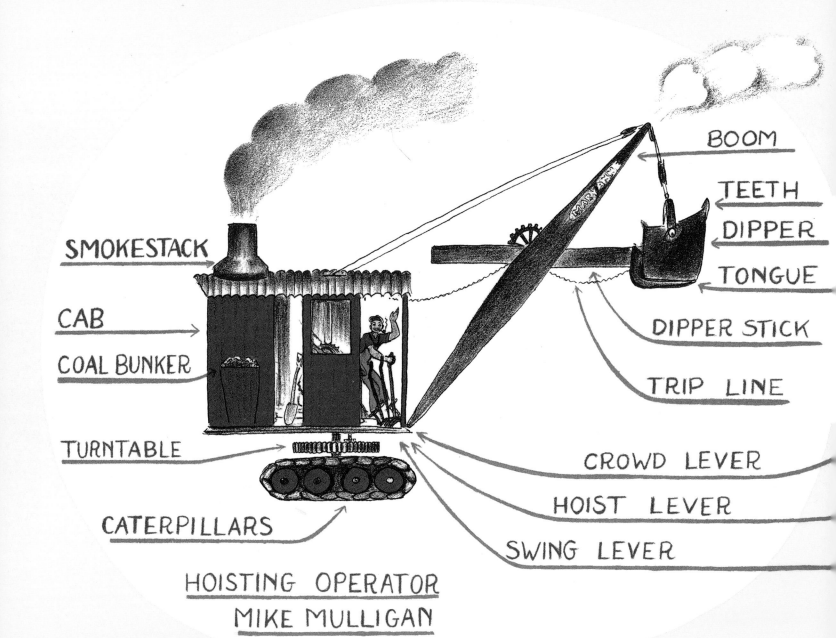

SMOKESTACK

CAB

COAL BUNKER

TURNTABLE

CATERPILLARS

HOISTING OPERATOR
MIKE MULLIGAN

BOOM

TEETH

DIPPER

TONGUE

DIPPER STICK

TRIP LINE

CROWD LEVER

HOIST LEVER

SWING LEVER

CROWD

HOIST

SWING

THE LITTLE HOUSE

STORY AND PICTURES
BY
VIRGINIA LEE BURTON

HOUGHTON MIFFLIN COMPANY · BOSTON

To
Dorgie

Once upon a time
there was a Little House
way out in the country.
She was a pretty Little House
and she was strong and well built.
The man who built her so well said,
"This Little House shall never be sold
for gold or silver and she will live to see
our great-great-grandchildren's
great-great-grandchildren living in her."

67

The Little House
was very happy
as she sat on the hill
and watched the countryside around her.
She watched the sun rise in the morning
and she watched the sun set in the evening.
Day followed day,
each one a little different
from the one before . . .
but the Little House stayed
just the same.

In the nights
she watched the moon grow
from a thin new moon to a full moon,
then back again to a thin old moon;
and when there was no moon
she watched the stars.
Way off in the distance
she could see the lights of the city.
The Little House was curious about the city
and wondered what it would be like to live there.

71

Time passed quickly
for the Little House
as she watched the countryside
slowly change with the seasons.
In the Spring,
when the days grew longer
and the sun warmer,
she waited for the first robin
to return from the South.
She watched the grass turn green.
She watched the buds on the trees swell
and the apple trees burst into blossom.
She watched the children
playing in the brook.

In the long Summer days
she sat in the sun
and watched the trees
cover themselves with leaves
and the white daisies cover the hill.
She watched the gardens grow,
and she watched the apples turn red and ripen.
She watched the children swimming in the pool.

In the Fall,
when the days grew shorter
and the nights colder,
she watched the first frost
turn the leaves to bright yellow
and orange and red.
She watched the harvest gathered
and the apples picked.
She watched the children
going back to school.

In the Winter,

    when the nights were long and the days short,
  and the countryside covered with snow,
she watched the children

coasting and skating.
  Year followed year. . . .
    The apple trees grew old
      and new ones were planted.
      The children grew up
        and went away to the city . . .
         and now at night
           the lights of the city
             seemed brighter and closer.

79

One day
the Little House
was surprised to see
a horseless carriage coming down
the winding country road. . . .
Pretty soon there were more of them
on the road and fewer carriages pulled by horses.
Pretty soon along came some surveyors and surveyed a line
in front of the Little House.
Pretty soon along came a steam shovel and dug a road
through the hill covered with daisies. . . .
Then some trucks came and dumped big stones on the road,
then some trucks with little stones,
then some trucks with tar and sand,
and finally a steam roller came
and rolled it all smooth,
and the road was done.

Now the Little House
watched the trucks and automobiles
going back and forth to the city.
Gasoline stations . . .
roadside stands . . .
and small houses
followed the new road.
Everyone and everything
moved much faster now than before.

More roads were made,
and the countryside was divided into lots.
More houses and bigger houses . . .
apartment houses and tenement houses . . .
schools . . . stores . . . and garages
spread over the land
and crowded around the Little House.
No one wanted to live in her
and take care of her any more.
She couldn't be sold for gold or silver,
so she just stayed there and watched.

Now it was not so quiet and peaceful at night.
Now the lights of the city were bright and very close,
and the street lights shone all night.
"This must be living in the city,"
thought the Little House,
and didn't know whether she liked it or not.
She missed the field of daisies
and the apple trees dancing in the moonlight.

Pretty soon
there were trolley cars
going back and forth
in front of the Little House.
They went back and forth
all day and part of the night.
Everyone seemed to be very busy
and everyone seemed to be in a hurry.

Pretty soon there was an elevated train
going back and forth above the Little House.
The air was filled with dust and smoke,
and the noise was so loud
that it shook the Little House.
Now she couldn't tell when Spring came,
or Summer or Fall, or Winter.
It all seemed about the same.

91

Pretty soon
there was a subway
going back and forth
underneath the Little House.
She couldn't see it,
but she could feel and hear it.
People were moving faster and faster.
No one noticed the Little House any more.
They hurried by without a glance.

Pretty soon they tore down
the apartment houses and tenement houses
around the Little House
and started digging big cellars . . . one on each side.
The steam shovels dug down three stories on one side
and four stories on the other side.
Pretty soon they started building up . . .
They built up twenty-five stories on one side
and thirty-five stories on the other.

Now the Little House only saw the sun at noon,
and didn't see the moon or stars at night at all
because the lights of the city were too bright.
She didn't like living in the city.
At night she used to dream of the country
and the field of daisies
and the apple trees
dancing in the moonlight.

The Little House
was very sad and lonely.
Her paint was cracked and dirty . . .
Her windows were broken and her shutters hung crookedly.
She looked shabby . . . though she was just as good a house as ever underneath.

Then one fine morning in Spring
along came the great-great-granddaughter
of the man who built the Little House so well.
She saw the shabby Little House, but she didn't hurry by.
There was something about the Little House
that made her stop and look again.
She said to her husband,
"That Little House looks just like the Little House
my grandmother lived in when she was a little girl,
only *that* Little House was way out in the country
on a hill covered with daisies
and apple trees growing around."

They found out it was the very same house,
so they went to the Movers to see
if the Little House could be moved.
The Movers looked the Little House all over
and said, "Sure, this house is as good as ever.
She's built so well we could move her anywhere."
So they jacked up the Little House
and put her on wheels.
Traffic was held up for hours
as they slowly moved her
out of the city.

101

At first
the Little House
was frightened,
but after she got used to it
she rather liked it.
They rolled along the big road,
and they rolled along the little roads,
until they were way out in the country.
When the Little House saw the green grass
and heard the birds singing, she didn't feel sad any more.
They went along and along, but they couldn't seem to find
just the right place.
They tried the Little House here,
and they tried her there.
Finally they saw a little hill
in the middle of a field . . .
and apple trees growing around.
"There," said the great-great-granddaughter,
"that's just the place."
"Yes, it is," said the Little House to herself.
A cellar was dug on top of the hill
and slowly they moved the house
from the road to the hill.

The windows and shutters were fixed
and once again they painted her
a lovely shade of pink.
As the Little House settled down
on her new foundation,
she smiled happily.
Once again she could watch
the sun and moon and stars.
Once again she could watch
Spring and Summer
and Fall and Winter
come and go.

Once again
she was lived in
and taken care of.

Never again would she be curious about the city . . .
Never again would she want to live there . . .
The stars twinkled above her . . .
A new moon was coming up . . .
It was Spring . . .
and all was quiet and peaceful in the country.

KATY
AND THE
BIG SNOW

STORY AND PICTURES
BY
VIRGINIA LEE BURTON

HOUGHTON MIFFLIN COMPANY BOSTON

To

Johnnnnnnnn

from Jinnnnnnnnn

55 HORSE POWER AT DRAWBAR

DIESEL ENGINE

5 SPEEDS FORWARD

2 SPEEDS BACKWARD

TURNS AROUND IN SAME PLACE

EQUIPMENT

CITY SHOES

COUNTRY SHOE

HYDRAULIC

BULLDOZER

"V" TYPE SNOW PLOW

Katy was a beautiful red crawler tractor.
She was very big and very strong
and she could do a lot of things.

Katy had a bulldozer
to push dirt around with.

Katy also had a snow plow
to plow snow with.

Katy belonged to the Highway Department
of the City of Geoppolis.

The Highway Department repaired the roads in the summer
and kept them clear of snow in the winter
so traffic could run in and out and around the city.

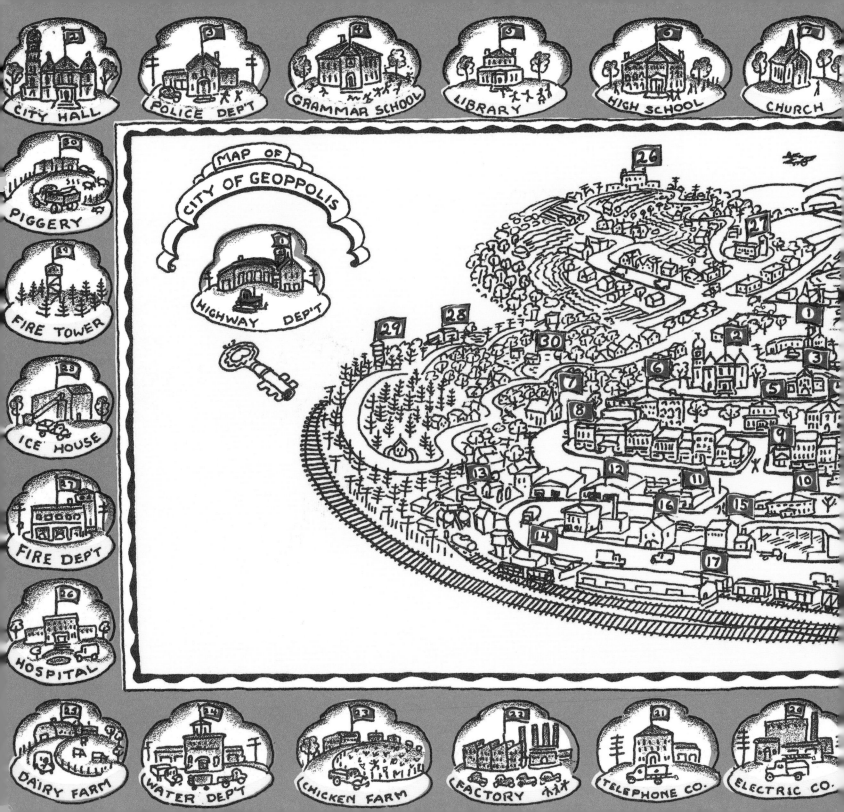

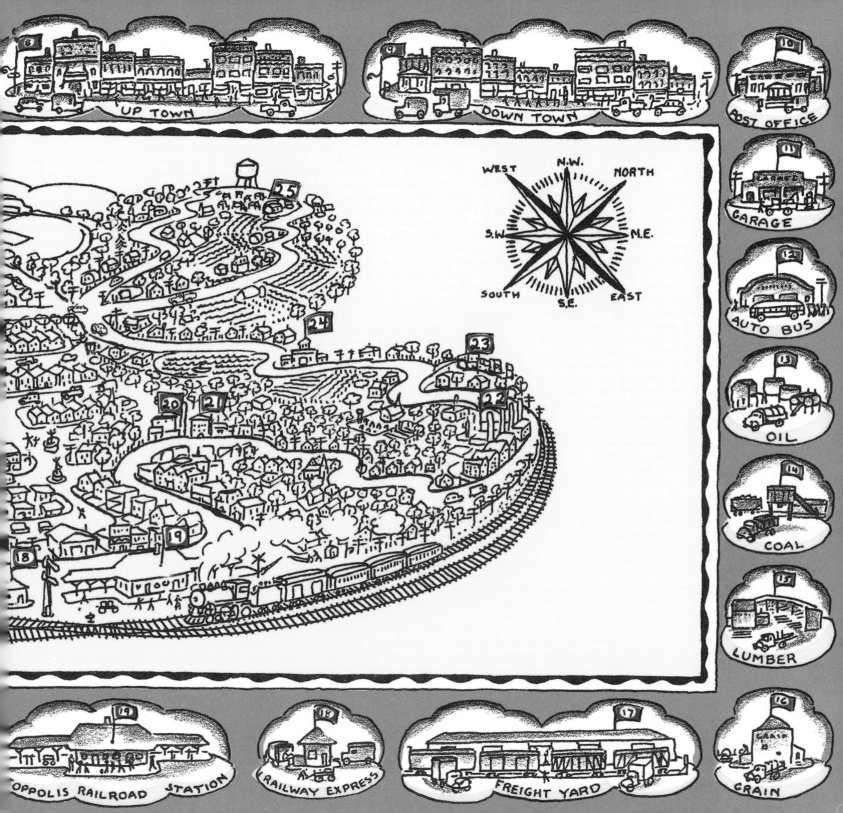

All summer Katy worked on the roads
with her bulldozer.
Katy liked to work.
The harder and tougher the job
the better she liked it.

Once when the steamroller fell in the pond
Katy pulled it out.
The Highway Department was very proud of her.
They used to say, "Nothing can stop her."

When winter came
they put snow plows
on the big trucks
and changed Katy's bulldozer
for her snow plow.

124

But Katy was so big and strong
she had to stay at home,
because there was not enough snow for her to plow.

Then early one morning it started to drizzle.
The drizzle turned into rain.
The rain turned into snow.
By noon it was four inches deep.
The Highway Department sent out the truck plows.

By afternoon the snow was ten inches deep
and still coming down.
"Looks like a Big Snow,"
they said at the Highway Department,
and sent Katy out.

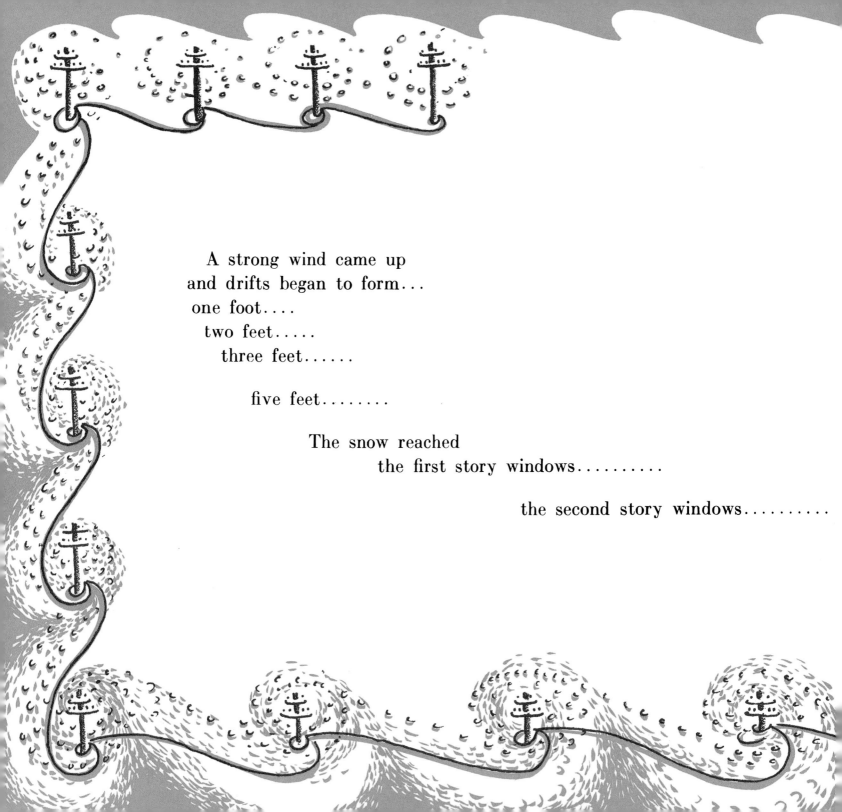

A strong wind came up
and drifts began to form...
one foot....
  two feet.....
    three feet......

      five feet.......

        The snow reached
              the first story windows..........

                    the second story windows..........

and then it stopped.
One by one the truck snow plows broke down....
The roads were blocked......
No traffic could move......
The schools, the stores, the factories were closed....
The railroad station and airport were snowed in....
The mail couldn't go through....
The Police couldn't protect the city....
The telephone and power lines were down...
There was a break in the water main...
The doctor couldn't get his patient to the hospital...
The Fire Department was helpless.....
Everyone and everything was stopped....
but...........

KATY

The City of Geoppolis was covered
with a thick blanket of snow.

Slowly and steadily
Katy started to plow out the city.

"Help!" called the Chief of Police.
"Help us to get out to protect the city."
"Sure," said Katy.   "Follow me."

So Katy plowed out the center of the city.

"Help," called out the Postmaster.
"Help us get the mail through."
"Sure," said Katy. "Follow me."

So Katy plowed down to the Railway Station.

"Help! Help!" called out the Telephone Company
and the Electric Company.
"The poles are down somewhere in East Geoppolis."
"Follow me," said Katy.

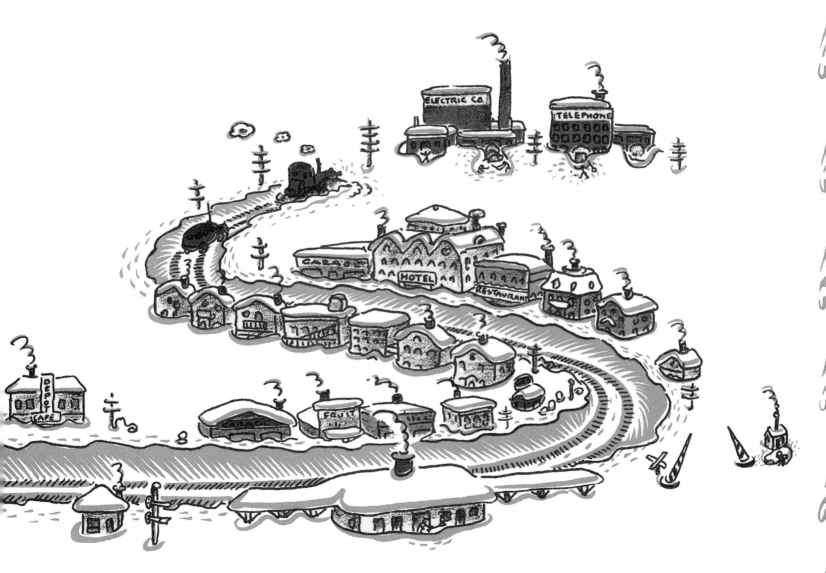

So Katy plowed out the roads to East Geoppolis.

"Help!"
called out the Superintendent of the Water Department.
"There's a break in the water main
somewhere in North Geoppolis."
"Follow me," said Katy

and she plowed out the roads to North Geoppolis.

"Help! Emergency!" called out the doctor.
"Help me get this patient to the hospital
way out in West Geoppolis."
"Sure," said Katy. "Follow me."

So Katy plowed out the roads to the hospital.

142

"Help! Help! Help!" called out the Fire Chief.
"There's a three alarm fire way out in South Geoppolis."
"Follow me," said Katy.

So Katy plowed out the roads to the fire in South Geoppolis.

144

On the way back a plane signalled for help.
The airport was snowed in.
Katy was beginning to get a little tired
but she wouldn't stop....
not Katy.

She hurried over to the airport
and plowed out the runways
so the airplane could land safely.

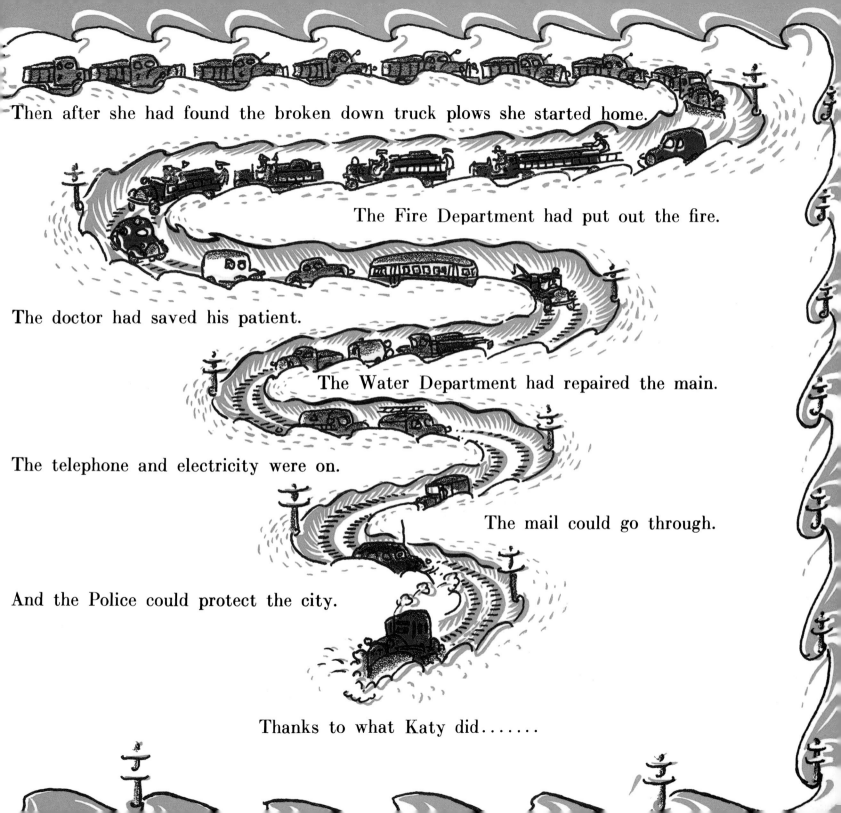

Then after she had found the broken down truck plows she started home.

The Fire Department had put out the fire.

The doctor had saved his patient.

The Water Department had repaired the main.

The telephone and electricity were on.

The mail could go through.

And the Police could protect the city.

Thanks to what Katy did.......

Katy finished up the side streets
so traffic could move in and out and around the city.
Then she went home to rest.
Then.....and only then did Katy stop.

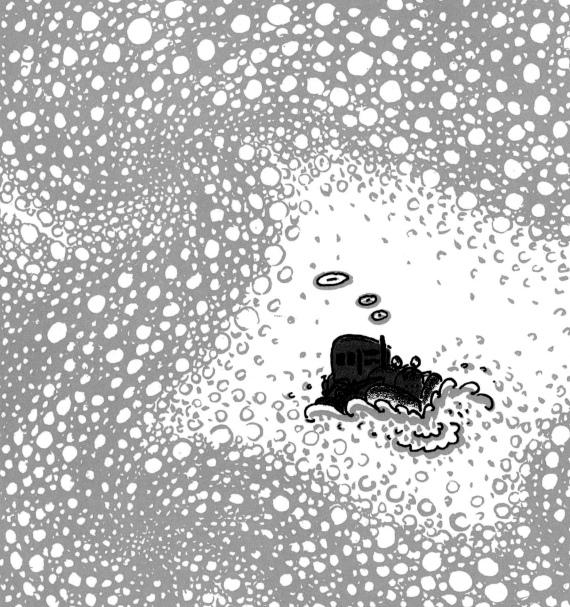

MAYBELLE

THE
CABLE CAR

BY
VIRGINIA LEE BURTON
HOUGHTON MIFFLIN CO.

Way out in the far Far West
there is a city of many hills...
a city with water on three sides round...
a bay city...a sea port...a gay city...a friendly city...
a city of flowers and cable cars
THE CITY OF SAN FRANCISCO.
To
the people of this city
who love their cable cars and
especially to MRS. HANS KLUSSMAN, leading light
in the fight to save them from extinction,
I dedicate this book

Foreword

The first of the cable cars was born in San Francisco August 1, 1873 . . . the invention of Andrew S. Hallidie. Born because Hallidie was fond of animals and could not bear to see the poor horses struggling and falling down when they tried to climb the steep hills which were so slippery when wet. So successful was the first cable car that soon there were many more . . . as many as eight different companies were formed and operated in San Francisco in the days before the earthquake and fire of 1906.

After the fire many of the cable lines were converted to electricity. Then as the city grew and changed

"Progress" in the form of streetcars, gasoline buses and trackless trolleys took over all but two of the remaining cable companies — The Municipal Railway Company, owned by the city, and the California Street Cable Railroad Company recently acquired by the city. For lack of space and to simplify matters I have used only the Municipal cable car, but the story of their survival is much the same.

For further information on cable car history I recommend *Cable Car Carnival* by Lucius Beebe and Charles Clegg, and if you want to know what makes them go read Frank Parker's *Anatomy of the San Francisco Cable Car*.

Maybelle was a cable car
    a San Francisco cable car
        Cling clang ... clingety clang
            Up and down and around she went.

GRIP AND LEVER

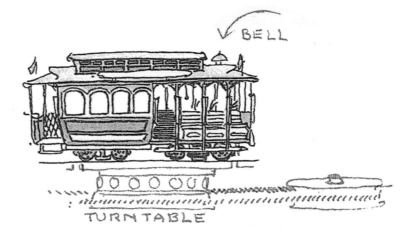

BELL

TURN TABLE

TRACK BRAKE AND LEVER

Maybelle had a bell on top
Ring two to go . . . and one to stop.
Underneath she had a grip
to grab the cable under the street.

She had three different kinds of brakes
one for the wheels . . . one for the track . . .
and an emergency brake to jam in the slot
so she could stop whenever she ought.

FRONT WHEEL BRAKES AND PEDAL
REAR WHEEL BRAKES AND LEVER

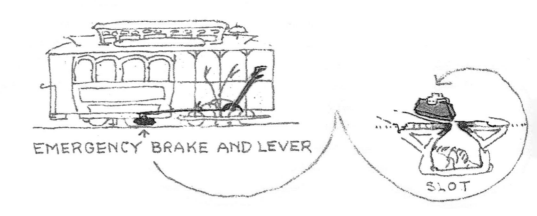

EMERGENCY BRAKE AND LEVER

SLOT

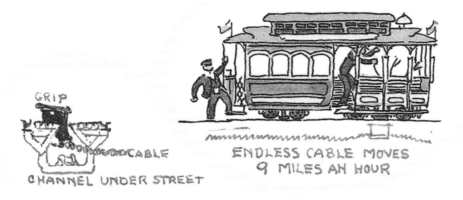

GRIP

CHANNEL UNDER STREET

ENDLESS CABLE MOVES
9 MILES AN HOUR

TING TING

GRIPMAN PULLING GRIP LEVER

Maybelle had a Gripman and a Conductor.
The Gripman pulled the levers
pushed the pedal and rang the bell
for Maybelle to stop or go.

The Conductor collected the fares
called out the streets and
helped with the rear wheel brakes
when the hills were very steep.

TING

GRIPMAN PULLING TRACK BRAKE LEVER

TING

CONDUCTOR WORKING REAR WHEEL
BRAKES. GRIPMAN PUSHING FOOT
PEDAL FOR FRONT WHEEL BRAKES.

TING

GRIPMAN PULLING EMERGENCY BRAKE ON

163

ELLIS

O'FARREL

GEARY

Fares please ... ting ting ... Let's go.

Not too fast ... and not too slow ...

Stop at the crossing ...

Wait for the light ...

POST

SUTTER

Then ride the cable

right up to the top ...

Stop ... and look at the view.

BUSH

PINE

CALIFORNIA

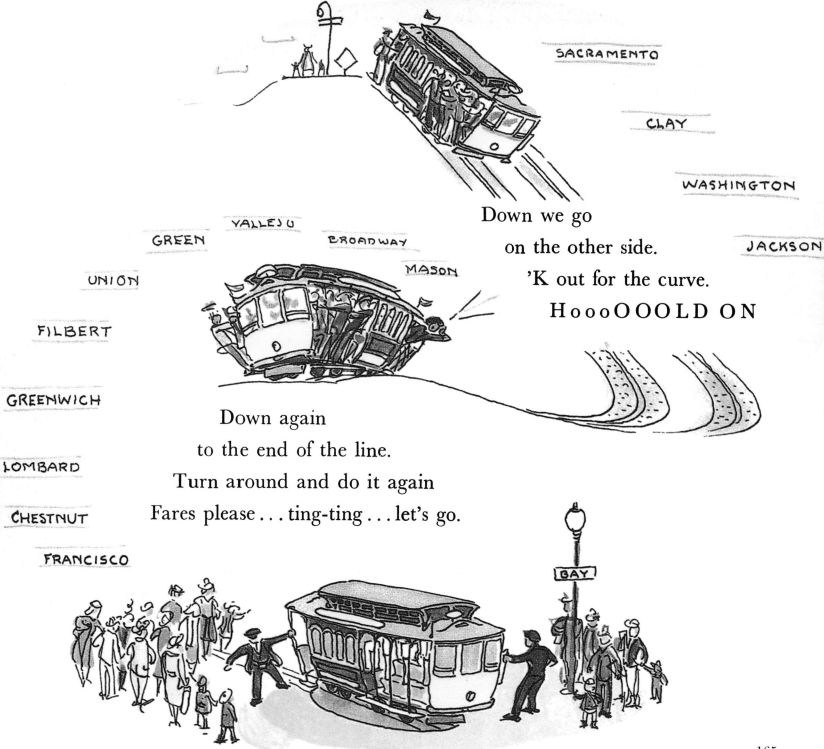

SACRAMENTO

CLAY

WASHINGTON

Down we go
on the other side.
'K out for the curve.

JACKSON

HoooOOOLD ON

VALLEJO

GREEN

BROADWAY

UNION

MASON

FILBERT

GREENWICH

Down again
to the end of the line.
Turn around and do it again
Fares please...ting-ting...let's go.

LOMBARD

CHESTNUT

FRANCISCO

BAY

No hill too steep...
no load too heavy...
Always cheerful...
and most polite...

She rang her gong
and sang her song
from early morn
till late at night.

BAY

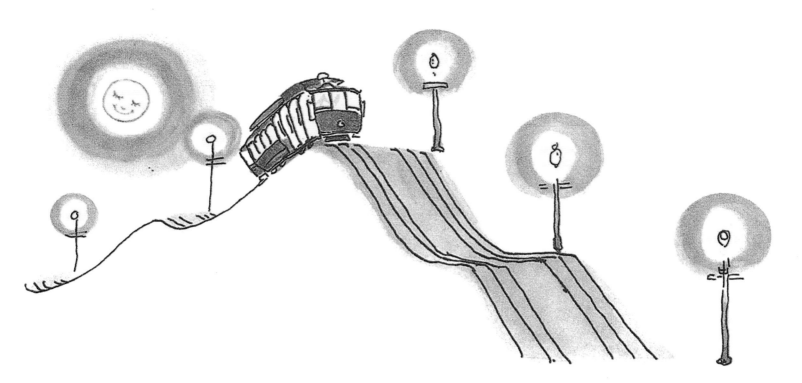

From late at night
to early morn...
Maybelle rested
with her sisters
in the big green barn.

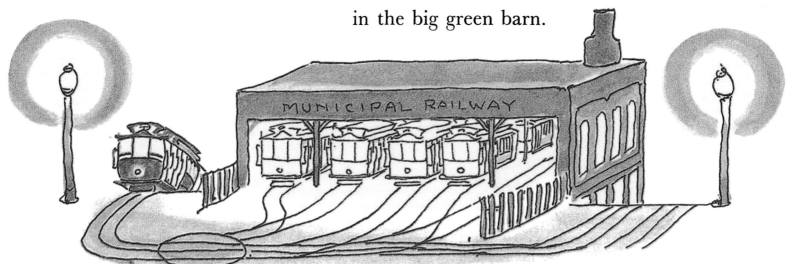

MUNICIPAL RAILWAY

Born in San Francisco long ago
they had watched their City change and grow,
the new come in and the old go out
while they remained the same.

At night while the City slept
they exchanged the news of the day
or played the game "Remember when..."
until it was time to go out again.

MUNICIPAL RAILWAYS

"Remember when the City was small
when everyone knew everyone else
and nobody hurried and nobody worried.
Those were the good old times.

"Remember when mansions crowned the hills
when our family was large and rich and famous,
the pride of the City and joy of the people.
Those were the gay old times.

"Remember the Sunday afternoon rides
out to the public parks and beaches
and the all-day outings on holidays.
Those were the merry old times."

They seldom remembered the terrible fire
which destroyed the City overnight.
Instead they remembered how quickly the City
rebuilt and grew some more.

They remembered when many of the cable lines
were changed into electric lines
and they remembered the first horseless carriage
and how people laughed and yelled "get a horse."

Now the streets were crowded with traffic
and everyone hurried and seemed to be worried.
Electric trolleys and gasoline buses had
replaced almost all of the old family lines.

Maybelle and her sisters worked for the City.
The City had been so busy growing
she had neglected her little cable cars
and they needed a new coat of paint.

Maybelle was always first out in the morning
and last to come in at night.
She loved her City . . . she loved her work
and most of all she loved the people.

MUNICIPAL RAILWAYS

Maybelle's hill was very steep
and very slippery when wet...
Even taxi cabs stayed off this hill
in damp or foggy weather...BUT

No hill too steep for Maybelle...
No matter the weather...wet or dry.
She could not slip...she had her grip
and three kinds of brakes besides.

TING! TING! TING!

When visitors came from the rest of the world

to see the sights of the City...they admired

the beautiful views...the two big bridges

the public buildings and parks and zoos

but what they liked the most of all

was to ride on a little cable car.

They paid no attention to the trolleys and buses
because they had plenty of those at home.

This made Big Bill, the bus,
just a bit jealous.
"After all," he boasted,
"I'm bigger and stronger
and newer and faster
and more economical."

His route ran by the City Hall
and he knew the City Fathers.

One day as Maybelle was going along

taking her time and singing her song

Big Bill honked his horn and hooted

"Out of my way...out of my way...

you little old cable car...

I just heard the City Fathers say

the cable cars must go...

that you're too old and out of date

much too slow and can't be safe...

and worst of all YOU DON'T MAKE MONEY.
What they want is Speed and Progress
and E-CON-O-MY . . . and that means US.
Ho ho . . . poor little old cable car . . .
Too bad you're not a bus,"
and he ground his gears
and shoved his way into traffic
leaving a trail of gasoline fumes
and Maybelle sad and unhappy.

"Oh me ... oh my ... oh dearie me ...
If this is true what shall we do.
Anyway I'd rather be me ...
a little old cable car
than a great big old ...
clumsy old ... stuffy old ...
and yes ... smelly old bus."
She said as she choked
on the gasoline fumes.

Of course she didn't say this out loud
because she was much too polite.

The rest of the day
seemed long and dreary
Maybelle's heart was
sad and weary...
The hills too high
the load too heavy
Her bell rang wrong.

DONG DING DING DONG

Soon the news leaked out from City Hall
what the City Fathers planned to do.

Some people said, "Too bad . . .
Hate to see them go . . . Progress, I suppose."
Others sighed and said, "We'll miss them . . . What a pity
for our City to lose her cable cars . . . We'll be like any city."
And one person said . . . "Why do we have to?
We, the people, are the City.
Why can't we decide?"

So they called a public meeting
in the Public Library
of all the friends of the cable cars
and called themselves

THE CITIZENS' COMMITTEE TO SAVE THE CABLE CARS.

Letters and telegrams
poured in from all over the world
begging the City Fathers to keep
the cable cars.

The Citizens' Committee stormed City Hall
demanding a chance for the people to vote,
to answer the question YES or NO,
SHALL THE CITY KEEP HER CABLE CARS?

186

"Pooh pooh,"
said the City Fathers,
"Just sentimental talk...besides
you need to have a petition
to put the question
on the ballot."

No sooner said than done.
The people signed a petition
and presented it to City Hall.

So the fate
of Maybelle and her sisters
was put on the ballot as Question One,
The Citizens' Committee got busy
with posters, parades
and publicity.

189

Every day there were speeches
and people started taking sides.
Some said "YES", and some said "NO"
but nobody said perhaps or maybe.

The "No" people had facts and figures
and the "Yes" people answered with more.
The "No" people made more noise
but the "Yes" people worked harder.

Big Bill, the bus, was sure he'd win

so late at night while the City slept

he crept out to practice climbing

Maybelle's hill . . . up and down . . .

stop . . . and start . . .

"Nothing to it," boasted Bill,

"What's all the fuss about this hill?"

Then came one damp and foggy night
when big Bill tried to stop half way down.
He slipped . . . he slid . . . he turned around.
"Whew, that was close," groaned Bill.
"I don't think I like this hill."

At last Election Day arrived
when the people would decide by vote
whether the cable cars would stay or go.
The polls opened at seven in the morning
and closed at eight at night.

194

THE POLLS ARE CLOSED

No more speeches...no more talking...
just one vote from each and everyone
and no one could tell what the answer
would be until the polls were closed
and all the votes counted.

The people stood around quietly and waited
for the votes to be counted . . . Maybelle waited . . .
Big Bill waited . . . the whole City waited
to see what the answer would be.

Nine o'clock...ten o'clock...eleven o'clock...midnight.

"Hurray," shouted the people. "The answer is YES.

The cable cars have won...three to one.

Hurray for the cable cars...Long may they live."

They gathered around Maybelle
and covered her with flowers.
They turned her around
and all climbed on.
"No fares please...
    Ting ting...let's go
        This ride's on me
            and free for all."

DING GA TI DING DING DING DING

It reminded Maybelle
of the "good old times"
when everyone knew
everyone else...
and life was gay
and friendly.

On her way back Maybelle met Big Bill.
"Congratulations," he honked, "I'm glad you won.
Your hill's too steep for me and
much too slippery when wet."
"Thank you," rang Maybelle,
"and let's be friends."

"Okay," said Bill, "and by the way
I just heard the new City Fathers say
that you and your sisters each would have
a new coat of paint...also they have named
one day each year to celebrate
as CABLE CAR DAY."

THANKYOU AGAIN..TING TING..AND GOODNIGHT

YOU'RE WELCOME..BEEP BEEP...BE SEEIN' YOU

Home went Maybelle . . . clingety clang . . .
Ringing her gong and singing her song.
Good news . . . ting ting . . . good news she sang
Our day's not done . . . it's just begun.